For my father, Hugh Antonsen

Printed in Italy.

First edition

1 2 3 4 5 6 7 8 9 10

Library of Congress Cataloging in Publication Data

Brown, Ruth.
   The big sneeze.

   Summary: A farmer sneezes a fly off his nose and
causes havoc in the barnyard.
   1. Children's stories, American. [1. Farm life—
Fiction. 2. Humorous stories] I. Title.
PZ7.B81698Bi 1985     [E]     84-23385
ISBN 0-688-04665-7
ISBN 0-688-04666-5 (lib. bdg.)

# THE BIG SNEEZE

## Ruth Brown

Lothrop, Lee & Shepard Books
New York

One hot afternoon, the farmer and his animals were dozing in the barn. The only sound was the buzz-buzz of a lazy fly.

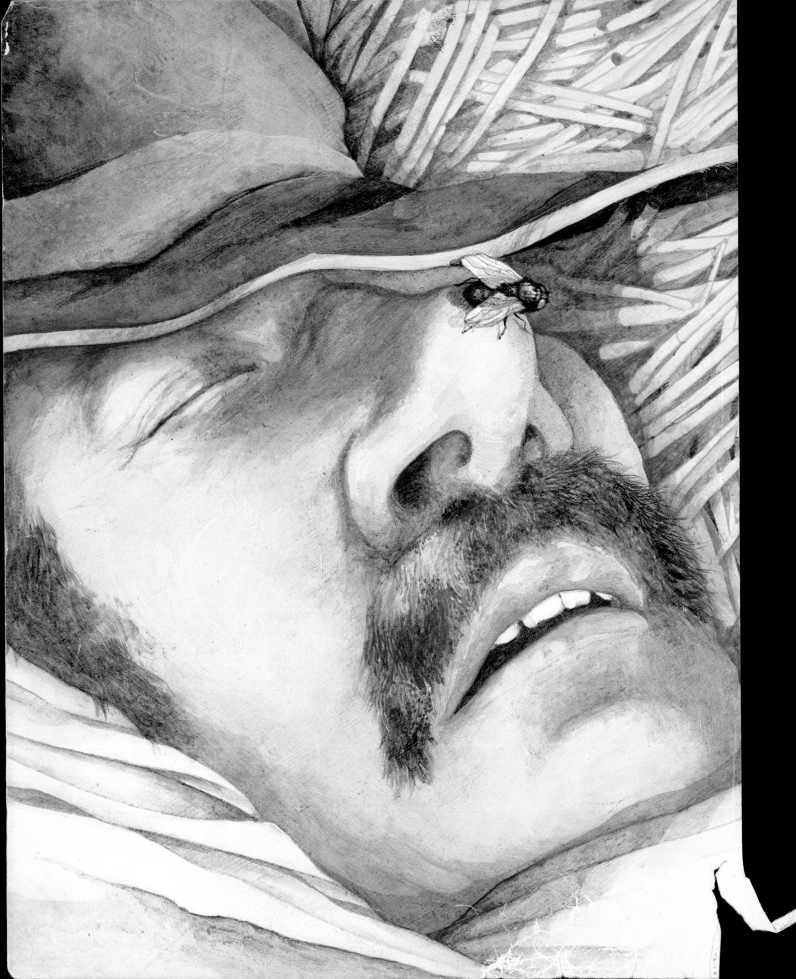

Suddenly the buzzing stopped –
the fly had landed right on the end of the farmer's nose!

"ATISHOOOOOOOOOOO!" the farmer sneezed so hard that the fly was blown high up into a spider's web.

This disturbed the spider,
who captured the fly –

which alerted the sparrow,
who chased the spider.

This wakened the cat,
who leapt at the bird –

which woke the dog,
and frightened the rats –

who fled from the barn,
chased by the dog –

which scattered the startled
hens from their roost –

and panicked the terrified donkey!

'What on earth have you done?'' shrieked the farmer's wife.

"Nothing, my dear," replied the farmer. "I only sneezed!"